什麼顏色？

What color?

Yu Jun Chen

樹梢上站著一隻鳥。

A bird was sitting on a branch.

他自由自在、快樂的在森林裡飛翔。

He lived happily and free in the forest.

有一天，森林裡傳來一陣歌聲。
One day, he heard a song echoing throughout the forest.

好奇一探，原來是一隻漂亮的三色鳥。

He was fascinated.
He followed the sound until he spotted a gorgeous bird.

那天以後,他開始覺得自己不美,很不快樂。

After seeing the gorgeous bird, he felt inferior. This made him very unhappy.

於是,他決定去尋找顏色。

He decided to find some new colors.

帶回來替自己染色。

To dye his feathers.

全部倒進大鍋子裡。

He poured colors into a big pot.

有一點奇怪……

It looked a bit strange...

跳進去!

The bird jumped into the pot.

他卻染了一片黑……

The dye covered him in black.

他更難過了,因為這不是他想要的樣子。

He became even more sad, because his plan failed.

突然，下雨了……

Suddenly, it began to rain...

他從地面的水中看見了自己的清晰倒影。

He saw his reflection in the water.

人生崎嶇的道路上，跌跌撞撞的這些經驗雖然會迷惘、失望，卻也讓我們一次又一次看得清晰自己的模樣。

Sometimes we hit rough patches in life. Even though we feel sad and lost, these experiences are chances to make us stronger and learn who we truly are.

獻給曾經迷惘的我們。

For those of us who used to be lost.

Yu Jun Chen

關於作者 About Yu Jun

1994年出生，因為父親的啟發，小時候就是個到處塗鴉、剪貼的重度成癮者。大學就讀美術系，2016年背起七公斤的背包，獨自出門一趟長途旅行，帶著樂天性格，走過16個國家，路上遇見太多人、事啟發，酸甜苦辣、好的壞的都成為人生中的養分。旅途之中受到一位陌生旅人的啟發，而找回畫圖熱情。因為不善文字、想說故事，比起畫一幅只掛在美術館或藝廊，看似遙不可及的畫，更希望能畫出與人們更貼近生活、有共鳴的作品，所以我成為一位插畫創作者，繼續到處冒險，增加視野，相信擁有富足的人生經驗，才能畫出扣人心弦的故事。

I'm an illustrator based in Taipei, Taiwan. In college I majored in Fine Arts with a specialty in oil painting. After I graduated, I took a long trip across 16 countries in Europe, and was inspired by the many unforgettable experiences on my trip.

Life is full of deep experiences, and as an artist I believe that creating meaningful stories is the best thing we can do with them.

什麼顏色？

What color?

作　　者／陳育均
出　　版／飛柏創意股份有限公司
　　　　　10446 台北市中山區林森北路 112 號 6 樓
　　　　　電話：02-2562-0026
　　　　　Email：service@flipermag.com
總 編 輯／賈俊國
副總編輯／蘇士尹
編　　輯／高懿萩
行銷企畫／張莉滎・廖可筠・蕭羽猜

發 行 人／何飛鵬
法律顧問／元禾法律事務所王子文律師
發　　行／布克文化出版事業部
　　　　　台北市中山區民生東路二段141號8樓
　　　　　電話：(02)2500-7008　傳真：(02)2502-7676
　　　　　Email：sbooker.service@cite.com.tw

台灣發行所／英屬蓋曼群島商家庭傳媒股份有限公司城邦分公司
　　　　　台北市中山區民生東路二段141號2樓
　　　　　書虫客服服務專線：(02)2500-7718；2500-7719
　　　　　24小時傳真專線：(02)2500-1990；2500-1991
　　　　　劃撥帳號：19863813；戶名：書虫股份有限公司
　　　　　讀者服務信箱：service@readingclub.com.tw
香港發行所／城邦(香港)出版集團有限公司
　　　　　香港灣仔駱克道193號東超商業中心1樓
　　　　　電話：+852-2508-6231　傳真：+852-2578-9337
　　　　　Email：hkcite@biznetvigator.com
馬新發行所／城邦(馬新)出版集團 Cité (M) Sdn. Bhd.
　　　　　41, Jalan Radin Anum, Bandar Baru Sri Petaling,
　　　　　57000 Kuala Lumpur, Malaysia
　　　　　電話：+603- 9057-8822　傳真：+603- 9057-6622
　　　　　Email：cite@cite.com.my
印　　刷／卡樂彩色製版印刷有限公司
初　　版／2018年(民107)05月
售　　價／360元
ISBN／978-986-9699-08-2

FLIPER　城邦讀書花園 www.cite.com.tw　布克文化 WWW.SBOOKER.COM.TW　chenyujun.com